All Books by Harper Lin

www.HarperLin.com

Valentine's Victim

❄

An Emma Wild Mystery
Book #4

by Harper Lin

This is a work of fiction. Names, characters, organizations,places, events, and incidents are either products of the author's imagination or are used fictitiously.

ISBN-13: 978-0993949562

ISBN-10: 0993949568

Contents

Recipes

Chapter 1

"Come on, Emma, it'll be fun."

My sister Mirabelle poked me in the ribs with her bony fingers.

"Ow, stop!" I cried.

I was lying on the couch still wearing my pyjamas in the middle of the day. Mom and Dad were at work, but I was taking an extended hiatus from my career as a singer...and celebrity. I was on strike. Eating ice cream, cupcakes and Doritos had been my full-time job for the past week.

"I don't even think you're in that much pain anymore," Mirabelle said. "I bet you're just using this as an excuse to eat more junk food."

"No," I said dramatically. "I'm really heartbroken. My life is this couch. Is there any more ice cream in the freezer?"

"I think there's only lemon sorbet."

"Boo. Sorbet sucks."

Mirabelle crossed her arms. "I just don't understand. This is a great opportunity for you to stuff your face with more sugary junk. And you get to be a judge. What's not to like?"

"People," I said. "I don't want to see people. Especially one particular person."

"I'll make sure he doesn't get on the premises."

We were referring to Detective Sterling Matthews. The bastard. I caught him making out with his partner Sandra at work a week ago. In his office too.

And to think I'd helped him solve a kidnapping case recently.

I covered my head with a blanket. Mirabelle yanked it down. Sometimes she was more like my mother than my older sister. She'd certainly been bossy growing up.

"The last time Sterling broke your heart, you went to New York and became famous. This time you're just going to sit around and do nothing while your phone rings off the hook?"

Everyone's been trying to get a hold of me, but I couldn't even bear the thought of checking who the messages were from or what they wanted. My manager Rod had been one of the more persistent callers, trying to pin me down for promotional duties for my third album. Representatives from my record company were probably peeved as well.

And don't get me started on my PR team. I also knew that Sterling was trying to get in touch and I didn't want to hear from him.

A week ago, I had caught Sandra on top of him when I visited him at his office. When I pounded on the door, he opened up and was completely speechless.

"I see that you've really moved on," I had said coldly.

Sandra had smirked in the background while buttoning her shirt back up. I'd noticed that her bra was hot pink. With her hair down, she'd looked even sexier.

"Is this what you've been doing while we were apart?" I asked.

Sterling shook his head. "Emma, we were just..."

"I saw what you were doing. And it looked like you were enjoying it too."

"No!"

"No?" Sandra raised her ever-arching eyebrow. "It didn't seem that way to me."

"We were just, uh..."

I'd never heard Sterling stutter before. Completely silent and brooding, yes, but guilty and stuttering, no.

"There's lipstick all over your face," I pointed out.

Sterling just blinked at me, looking stupid with all that pink gunk smeared all around his lips. Some sounds came out of his mouth, but they weren't coherent words. I looked back at him with what was probably a hurt expression.

"I came here to tell you that I chose you," I snapped, "but you obviously chose someone else."

Sandra was smoothing her hair back into a neat bun and she smiled at me in her usual patronizing way. I'd never seen Sandra with makeup on before. She must've gotten gussied up once in a while to seduce Sterling. I wanted to smack both of them, but I resisted.

Instead, I turned on my heel and stormed out.

Sterling didn't even run out after me, so I figured there was nothing more he could say.

I guess I didn't know Sterling as well as I thought I did after all. We had been high school sweethearts until we graduated. Then he broke up with me, and I was crushed.

Long story short, I moved to New York, became a singer, dated a few famous and not-so-famous men, and then finally fell in love for the second time in my life with Nick Doyle, the movie star. We even lived together for four years, but we broke up because we were both working and traveling too much. I had wanted to get married, settle down and have children, and at the time Nick didn't.

This past Christmas, I had decided to take a break from recording and touring to spend time with my family. Here in Hartfield, my hometown in Ontario, I reconnected with Sterling again and we started seeing each other. I thought that we were returning to the passionate romance we used to have as teenagers.

But now I was starting to think that Sterling could have passionate romances with anyone. At least Nick only faked it with his leading ladies. Sure, he had dated his share of beauties before we were together, but he was always the monogamous type, despite how the press tried to portray him to be.

Sterling tried to get in touch with me the day after I caught him, but I was too sick to my stomach to see him and listen to his lame excuses. He even came around once, but I told my parents to tell him to scram.

While I avoided Sterling, I also managed to ignore my manager Rod and everybody else trying to book me for promotional appearances, interviews and performances for my third album release on Valentine's Day. I had responsibilities, and this was the first time in my life that I actively avoided them.

All I wanted to do was to hide. I'd spent most of my twenties in the music industry. I was only supposed to be taking a short break over the holidays, but I had extended it to February. Would this still be considered a quarter-life crisis if I was almost thirty?

Mirabelle poked me in the ribs again.

"You've got to go outside," she said. "Get some fresh air for God's sake."

"It's freezing outside," I said.

I knew I was being whiney, but I couldn't help it. I thought I was over being the vulnerable girl so sensitive to failed romances. My songs were all about heartbreak and I was sick of singing those songs. For my fourth album, I would record happier songs, reinvent myself. Right now, I just didn't feel up to it. I didn't feel up for anything.

Being a celebrity didn't make you immune to heartbreak. The industry was tough, love was tough, the whole world was tough and the safest I felt was inside my parents' home in Hartfield.

"Really, Emma." Mirabelle rolled her eyes. "It drives me crazy looking at you in that robe and those lame bunny slippers. Just get off your ass. Be one of the judges for the baking contest, get involved in something. It'll get you out of yourself, then you can go back to writing those happy songs that you were so excited about last week."

I grunted, then turned away from her on the couch.

"Also, do you want to throw me a baby shower?"

"A baby shower?" That got my attention. "You're due next month and we haven't had a shower yet, that's right."

"So can you plan it?"

Gingerly, I sat upright. I'd been watching trashy reality TV shows all day and my brain and body both felt like mush.

"Of course I'll do it," I said with some excitement. "You're right. I have been dwelling on this whole Sterling thing too much. I definitely need to get out of this slump."

"I thought it would be good for you," Mirabelle said. "Since you don't want to go back to work yet and you don't even want to go outside, you need something to keep you busy."

"There are loads of cheesy baby shower games we can do," I said, the gears in my head turning. "It won't be one of those lame baby showers. It'll be fun and it'll have plenty of alcohol!"

"Great," said Mirabelle. "Except that I can't drink."

"It'll have plenty of apple juice!" I said.

"Now are you going to be a judge for this contest or what?" Mirabelle asked.

Hartfield was holding its third annual baking contest this weekend. Mirabelle, the owner the Chocoholic Cafe, which was the most popular cafe in town, was a sponsor of the event. The contest

13

was open to all Hartfield residents except for professional bakers. The other two judges were one of the bakers who worked for Mirabelle, and another who worked in the supermarket's bakery section.

The contest lasted all weekend. The first round on Saturday required all the entrants to bring in cupcakes for a blind taste test. The best four entrants would move on to the next round, which required them to bake a cake on site on Sunday. The cakes were judged for taste, originality and presentation.

I did want to participate. My sister knew me well. It was exactly the kind of thing I wanted to do. I would've been more excited about it if I hadn't been in such a strange, hermetic mood lately. But Mirabelle was right—I had to take action to snap myself out of this depression. I couldn't let one guy get me down. Wasn't that what I sang about in one of my songs? I had to walk the walk.

"Right," I said, stretching my arms out. "I will be a judge for this baking contest. Count me in. Now if you'll excuse me, I'll be taking a long, hot shower."

"Atta girl," Mirabelle said. "Good idea. You were starting to develop some serious B.O."

Before I could make it up the stairs, the doorbell rang. I froze, afraid that it was Sterling.

Chapter 2

I made silent gestures to Mirabelle for her to get the door, but she simply shook her head, insisting that I do it.

I looked through the peephole. It was a guy who looked vaguely familiar. He wore chunky black glasses and was shivering in a hooded winter coat. Tentatively, I opened the door.

"Can I help you?" I asked.

"Hi, I'm Aaron Sanders, writer from *Rolling Stone*. I'm looking for Emma Wild?"

That was how I knew him. Shoot. A journalist in my home when I was in such a dishevelled state?

"I'm Emma Wild," I said.

Aaron gave me a quick once-over.

"Oh," he said. "Of course."

He flashed his own embarrassed smile. He probably had an image of me as a femme fatale, since the cover shoot for the magazine had been film noir-themed with lots of heavy shadows and sultry makeup.

"I look like crap without makeup," I said. "Print that if you want."

"No, you look beautiful," he said, mustering as much sincerity as he could.

"I don't mind," I said. "Maybe it'll make it easier for young girls who look up to me to know that. I hate it when they Photoshop me in pictures. But where are my manners? Come on in."

He stomped the snow off his boots on the Welcome mat and stepped in, still shivering. "I don't know if you remember me, but I interviewed you last year."

"Yes, of course I do. It was for that profile."

"It was pretty quick."

"I remember everyone who interviews me." I did too. At least their faces. Their names were much harder to recall. "Would you like some tea? And I think we have some homemade creamy zucchini soup if you're hungry."

"That would be great," Aaron said. "Sure is cozy in this town. It's a long way from Los Angeles."

"You're from L.A.? I love that city. I've been meaning to go back."

Aaron was so cold that it took him a while to take off his coat. What did you expect from a Californian? He was in his early thirties, with a slight bald patch. I had done a quick Q&A with him when I was doing a flurry of interviews in a hotel in Los Angeles a couple of years ago to promote my second album. He seemed okay. His write-up hadn't been so bad, but he didn't kiss my ass either. Some journalists were nice to your face, but wrote scathing things once they were back at their desks.

"I'm sorry to intrude on you in your home," he said. "But as you know, the issue with you on the cover is going to print in a couple of weeks and we still don't have an interview. Your manager said the best thing to do was to catch you down here. He said you weren't answering your phone."

"I have been sort of M.I.A.," I admitted. "I'm sorry about that. I'm recovering from...an illness."

"Oh. I'm sorry to hear that. Are you okay?"

"Yes. It was the flu." I faked a couple of coughs. "Almost over it. Sorry that you had to come all the way down here."

Aaron chuckled. "Canadians do apologize a lot, don't they?"

"Yes, we do," I said. "Sorry about that. I haven't been in the right state to talk to anyone, but I'm feeling much better now. Might be able to return to work soon too."

"I understand," he said. "I had the flu last year too. It was horrible. I thought I was going to die."

We went into the kitchen, where I put the kettle on for some tea. Mirabelle came in and introduced herself.

"So, are you staying somewhere in Hartfield, Aaron?" Mirabelle asked.

"Yes, I'm staying at the Sweet Dreams Inn."

The Sweet Dreams Inn was fit for a grandmother. It was all floral wallpaper, porcelain plates and crocheted afghans. It had been taken over by new management recently, by a Japanese couple in their late forties.

"Charming place," I said.

Except that it was rumored to be haunted, and the owner was murdered there by her son's girlfriend on New Year's Eve. But I didn't tell that to Aaron.

"Yes." Aaron chuckled. "Charm is the right word. I hope it's okay that I'll be following you around this weekend."

"Sure," I said.

I wasn't thrilled about it, but I supposed this was my punishment for not returning my manager's calls.

"What's a typical day like for you here?" asked Aaron.

"Well, since I'm feeling better now, I'm going to be throwing a baby shower for Mirabelle."

"Not just that," Mirabelle said. "She's judging the annual Hartfield baking contest this weekend."

Aaron smiled. "A baking contest?"

"Yes," I laughed. "Very quaint, I know. The first round is cupcakes."

"I can see why you like living here. You usually live in New York, right?"

"Yes."

"But you recently broke up with Nick Doyle. Was that why you moved?"

I laughed off his question. Part of my media training with my PR people was that whenever someone asked a personal question, you had to try to laugh it off as if it was the silliest thing ever you've ever heard.

"No, I still live in New York. Why wouldn't I? Hartfield is just where my family is."

"And what about Nick?" Aaron pressed. "How's he doing? Is it true that he'd been in Hartfield to visit you recently?"

I fake laughed again. Aaron was a nice guy – many journalists were – but it was his job to ask the questions the readers wanted to know the answers to, so I couldn't blame him. Not too much anyway.

"He's on a shoot right now in Morocco is what I know."

"We never got official word whether you were broken up or not."

I smiled sweetly. "I really can't talk about Nick. We have an agreement never to talk about each other to the press, to keep some semblance of privacy, you know?"

"So you are still together," Aaron said.

He had me cornered.

Were Nick and I together? I didn't know. Now that Sterling and I were over, I didn't know if Nick still wanted to be with me. Maybe there was truth in the rumor that he was cozying up with his co-star Chloe Vidal, the twenty-two-year-old blonde bombshell who was the latest It girl in Hollywood. Their photos were splashed all over the Internet. In one of them, they were having ice cream together on the streets of Morocco. I just hoped that Aaron wouldn't want to bring that up. I was barely over Sterling with Sandra.

"Oh, Aaron." I smiled mysteriously and shook my head in a teasing way. "You're just going to have to ask him. Anyway, you're from *Rolling Stone*, not *People*. Shouldn't we be talking about what really matters?"

"Politics?" He joked.

I mock rolled my eyes. "Of course not. The music."

This got the ball rolling on talking about my third album, about the producers I worked with, my vision and my influences. But as I spoke, I thought about what a pain it was going to be to have a journalist following me around in my hometown. It was my fault for taking the battery out of my cell phone. I could've given a phone interview if I would've known.

Chapter 3

After Aaron left, I breathed a sigh of relief. I'd dealt with worse, and he wasn't so bad, but I didn't like the feeling of being watched all the time. You'd think I'd be used to it by now.

"How exciting," Mirabelle said. "A *Rolling Stone* writer following you around."

I shrugged. "I wish he wouldn't."

"You've got nothing to hide."

"Except my personal life, which they always want to know about."

"What is going on anyway? I'm your sister and I don't even know. So are you going to get back together with Nick?"

I plopped back down on the couch and sighed.

"I don't know. He wrapped his film, but he hasn't tried to get in touch or anything. Maybe that's over too."

"Do you want to be with Nick?"

I shrugged again, trying to look nonchalant about it. Sure I did, but he had probably moved on.

Mirabelle could tell I didn't want to talk about it, so she changed the subject.

"Well, instead of choosing between boys, you get to choose between baked goods."

"You're probably right. The contest will be fun tomorrow. However, I've been packing on the pounds. I'll have to get back to my intense exercise regime soon."

I got up from the couch, feeling my stomach jiggle. Whenever I gained weight, it all went to my stomach. It was easier to hide under loose-fitting shirts, but my work required sexy, tight-fitting dresses.

"Sure is hard to be a celebrity," Mirabelle teased. "I've got to go home for dinner, but I'll pick you up tomorrow for the bake-off."

"Good night."

I went upstairs and took that long overdue shower and felt refreshed.

When I got out of the bathroom, I listened to some Ella Fitzgerald in my room and relaxed for a while.

After a week of incubation, trashy TV, heartbreak and boredom, my life was getting back its motion again. Things were speeding up all around me. The reporter, the bake-off, and the baby shower. Okay, so it wasn't exactly a lot. Not compared with my work life. Touring really took a toll on you. So did interviews and photo shoots and walking the red carpet. Not to mention getting chased by the paparazzi in your sweats.

I took out my notebook and started writing down ideas for Mirabelle's baby shower. I would invite only our closest female friends and hold it at this house. I'd make a banner that was a cutout of a baby-bottle with spilt milk. "Mirabelle's Baby Shower" would be written in the milk. There should be at least five baby shower games, like *who could suck the beer out of the baby bottle fastest and guess the mystery chocolate in a diaper taste test.*

Planning this baby shower excited me more than talk show appearances, awards parties and photo shoots that I was beginning to wonder when I'd ever want to go back to work.

By nature, I was simply a creative person. The celebrity thing was never really a goal. I had always wanted to sing and create. And now, I wanted to make the invitations to the shower by hand. I was pretty good at paper crafts, and I planned on making a pop-up card, where a baby would be springing out of a card shaped like an egg when the egg opened up.

In the back of my closet, I found my old box of craft supplies. There were construction paper, tape, stickers, doilies, goggly eyes and all sorts of other random knick-knacks that I had kept from when I used to do crafts when I was young. And by young, I meant up to my late teens.

Even now, I thought that if given a piece of paper and some scissors, I'd be happy for hours. I was a big kid at heart, which was why I wanted to have kids of my own soon.

In two hours, I managed to get eight invitations finished. I drew different expressions on each baby's face for a personal touch.

Mirabelle was going to have a son, but she wanted the shower to be gender-neutral. She didn't believe that only girls liked pink and boys liked blue. She wanted to be an open-minded parent and raise her son without conditioned gender preconceptions, so she didn't mind if we bought "girly" toys or pink things.

She felt this way because she had been a tomboy growing up but was reprimanded for liking boy's toys, which she thought had been unkind of my parents.

I wondered if I was going to have children of my own anytime soon. For a while there, I imagined myself marrying Sterling, settling down in Hartfield, being a stepmom to his two little girls, and having more kids of our own.

But now it looked like I would have to start at square one. I hadn't heard from Nick, even though his film shoot had wrapped. Maybe now that he was back in his Hollywood lifestyle of film shoots and press junkets, settling down with a family didn't matter as much as he claimed it did. My fears were probably realized: he had been chased me only when I had broken up with him. Playing hard to get – even though I wasn't playing – could get a guy to do crazy things sometimes. Maybe after some time away from me, he finally came to his senses.

I sighed as I made my ninth baby card. For now, I would just play with Mirabelle's baby and live the family life vicariously through her. She did the same thing with my celebrity lifestyle, enjoying the perks like attending parties with me sometimes and staying in posh hotels. Maybe I could just enjoy playing with a cute baby without all the work that came along with being a mother.

The thought cheered me up when the doorbell rang again. I hoped it wasn't Aaron, back with another load of questions about my love life.

I went downstairs, still wearing my fluffy purple robe and matching slippers. Nobody else was in the house. It was Friday, Mom and Dad's date night, when they wined and dined and enjoyed each other's company. It was sweet really. No wonder their marriage had lasted over thirty-five years.

I looked through the peephole again.

Yikes.

It was Sterling, looking really handsome even through the warped peephole.

"Emma," he said. "I know you're there. Can you please open up?"

"Just because I'm here doesn't mean I have to do anything," I said.

"Please, it's been a week. Can we talk?"

"Talk about what?" I said.

"About – you know what about."

I flung the door open, not even caring that my red hair was still wet, or that I wasn't wearing anything underneath my robe. Since Sterling was intruding on my time in my space, he would have to deal with it.

His eyes widened at the sight of me, and then he looked away when he found himself staring.

"May I come in?" he said.

"Fine. But you're not getting any tea or coffee."

He stepped in. His coat was covered with snow-flakes and I resisted the urge to wipe them off, as I would have in the past.

Sterling sat on the couch, which made me avoid it. I sat on the sofa instead.

"So talk," I said.

"About last week," he started uncomfortably. "It isn't what you think. Sandra and I were not getting hot and heavy in the office all the time. That day, she closed the doors and the curtains and just sort of started kissing me."

"Out of nowhere, she started kissing you? Isn't that considered sexual harassment or something?"

"Yes, well, I admit I wasn't entirely innocent. I didn't exactly fight her off."

"Right. I noticed. You looked quite comfortable from what I could tell."

Sterling sighed. "I don't know what to say. This might sound really lame, but I was under a lot of stress that week."

"And you wanted to blow off some steam?"

"Sure, we get along and she flirts with me sometimes, and she is attractive, but I want to be with you. I have to admit it was difficult when I couldn't see you last month. It was a blow to the ego that you had to think about whether you wanted to be with me or your ex-boyfriend. I thought about it and I know that you're ultimately going to choose Nick. He was the one who left town."

"You said you were willing to give me the space. I had just gotten out of a breakup and I was confused."

"So was I," Sterling said. "I just felt rejected, and when Sandra was showing me attention, I was flattered. I know it's no excuse, but..."

He didn't know what else to say. This was what was so aggravating about Sterling sometimes. He had a difficult time verbalizing how he felt. He was hurt because of the whole situation with Nick, and he took solace in the first brunette co-worker that shoved her cleavage in his face.

And I wasn't having it.

"Look Sterling, I know this was a difficult situation, but I'm looking for someone who wants to be with me and only me. You said that you did, but your actions say that you don't believe we have a chance. And I'm starting to think that we don't either. I'm looking for someone who's secure with himself and won't hook up with floozy co-workers if things are not going well in his relationship."

"Emma, I'm an idiot. I didn't think I had a chance."

"You said you were going to fight for me this time. But you never do." I shook my head. "No, I can't see us working out in the long-term. Being hurt by you once is enough."

Sterling's expression dimmed. "It's not as if Nick is innocent. You don't think he's with his co-star?"

I pressed my lips together and didn't answer.

"Just because you've never caught him, doesn't mean that he's been loyal."

I met Sterling's grey eyes. I couldn't believe that he would deflect this to Nick.

"This has nothing to do with Nick," I said. "Whatever he's doing doesn't concern me. I never said that we were together. Maybe he is with his co-star now, or maybe not. But when we were together, he was always faithful to me. I know that."

Nick just wasn't the type to cheat. Sure, other woman wanted him to, but he had been raised well. Nick was a mama's boy and treated women with respect.

Now that I thought about it, Sterling's parents divorced because his father had skipped out on the family to be with another woman. Did the apple fall far from the tree? Sterling was also divorced. Maybe he didn't know the first thing about how to make a marriage work.

I just couldn't risk giving up my career to be with someone who might not be worth it in the end.

"I'm sorry, Sterling. It's over. I hope you're happy with Sandra. I think you two have more in common anyway."

"Emma..."

I looked at him again expectantly, but he had nothing to add to that.

"I guess it was never meant to be anyway," Sterling finally said. "You have this huge career, and I'm just a small town detective. It was never going to work."

I nodded coldly. "It wasn't. You're right."

He stood up and made his way to the door. I sat where I was and watched him leave without another word.

When he left, I allowed myself to cry.

Chapter 4

B y the time Saturday rolled around, I was in a much better mood. If I weren't a judge, maybe I would've even entered the bake-off. Baking was relaxing, but I hadn't had much time to do that for the last few years. Once in a blue moon, Nick and I used to bake apple pies together in our New York apartment. In fact, Nick had done a lot of baking with his mother growing up, which I always thought was sweet.

The first round of the contest was in the early afternoon. The contestants brought their cupcakes to Hartfield High's gym, which was set up with tables, and the judges would just have to taste them and announce the four finalists. The rest of the day would be spent socializing and eating the rest of the cupcakes.

Mirabelle picked me up in front of the house. She was looking pretty classy in a black knitted dress under her black winter coat. We drove off to the high school. The reason the contest took place there was because they had a cooking classroom with six ovens that we could use for the Sunday portion of the contest when the finalists had to bake on the premises.

Aaron was already waiting for us in front of the high school when we pulled up. He was sipping from an extra large cup of coffee, from the Chocoholic Cafe no less. Mirabelle approved.

"What's that you have there?" she asked him.

"The Chocolate Americano," Aaron said. "I'd never had a Chocolate Americano before."

"It was Emma's invention," Mirabelle said proudly.

"Really?" It was the most impressed I'd ever seen Aaron. "This is amazing. Grammy winner and coffee genius."

"You just add some chocolate to it," I said. "No biggie. Adding chocolate to anything makes it better."

"Hence, the Chocoholic Cafe," said Mirabelle.

"Genius family," said Aaron.

The three of us went inside the gym, where many of the long tables were already full of cupcakes.

"We're going to try all these?" I exclaimed. There were at least forty contestants.

This was my first bake-off at Hartfield. They only started this tradition three years ago, and I'd missed every single one of them. Part of the reason

I wanted to stay in town was probably to do stuff like this, which I never got to do anymore.

Aaron must've read my mind.

"No wonder you don't want to go back to New York," he joked.

When all the contestants sat down, Mirabelle went up to make her opening speech.

"Welcome to the third annual Hartfield Bake-off. It's a privilege to have you all here today. As you know, the winner receives a romantic getaway to Hawaii for two, courtesy of our sponsor, Sunstream Travel. You'll also get the coveted Chocoholic Cafe VIP card, which is good for one year's worth of free hot chocolate from my cafe."

The crowd cheered. She introduced the judges, and we each got up on stage. People snapped pictures, and a few people screamed my name, but this was a mild audience compared to my sold-out concerts. The pictures might end up in the town paper, although they could make their way to the tabloids and the Internet. I didn't mind too much, except the execs at my record company might be upset to see that I'd chosen cupcakes over promoting my new album.

The contestants were all of different ages, and there were almost as many males as females. I had assumed it was going to be mostly old ladies, but I was wrong. My dad wanted to enter, but he couldn't because there was a judge in the family, not to mention Mirabelle was also a sponsor.

Mirabelle announced that we would be doing our first round of blind taste tests soon. They had to start preparing their entries by cutting their cupcakes into four pieces, placing them on a tray and writing their entry number on the blank tag that they were given to put in front of the cupcake.

After that, we tried over forty cupcake samples. Not all at once of course. We each tried five at a time, and selected the two we liked the most within the five. That we did eight times until we had our top sixteen. Then the judges compared notes. The cupcakes that were favored by two or more of the judges got a pass into the top eight. If we disagreed, we had to try the ones the other judges picked and decide on the best ones collectively.

Once we had our top eight cupcakes, then we really got down to business in choosing the top four. Most of the cupcakes were delicious. Each judge had their preferences in regards to flavor. I loved red velvet, and the other judge, Mike, who was Mirabelle's baker, was an expert in anything chocolate. The third judge, Sylvia, preferred anything original. The lavender cupcake got her vote.

Some were dry, some were ultra light, some were heavy on cream, some were enormous and some were half the size of what cupcakes should be. In the end, we chose four great cupcakes: vanilla, strawberry, lavender, and chocolate Oreo. They didn't taste artificial, the frostings were rich and the cakes were moist but fluffy.

When we announced the winners, they went up the stage to receive their finalist ribbons.

Lena Mumson, a brunette in her thirties, looked very smug about the win. She had made the scrumptious lavender cupcakes with the lemon frosting.

Cherry Anderson, a pretty girl with honey blond corkscrew hair, had made the fresh-tasting strawberry cupcakes with fresh strawberries sticking out on top of the whipped cream frosting. She grinned from ear to ear as she bounced up the stage.

Demi Lauriston, a bottled blonde, had made the vanilla cupcake. She went up the stage carrying her youngest son in her arms. I gave the boy's little hand a high five when he passed by.

Larson Davies, a slightly tubby man in his mid-thirties, had made the chocolate Oreo cupcakes, to my surprise. He wore a soccer jersey and looked too athletic to be the baking type. His Oreo cupcakes were amazing. There was even a "surprise" melted Oreo at the bottom of the cupcake.

The four posed for a picture together after shaking our hands. Cherry had squealed when she shook my hand, saying that "Cornflower Blues" was a favorite song of hers and that she loved me. I gave her a hug.

"So that's our final four," Mirabelle said into the mic. "They'll be back tomorrow afternoon for the final cake bake-off. Remember, a romantic getaway to Hawaii is in the stakes, as well as free hot chocolate for a year! Now let's divide up the rest of the cupcakes and share them amongst the crowd. Let's party!"

After some mingling and pats on the backs, the finalists went home to prepare their recipes for tomorrow's contest. All except Lena, who stayed and mingled with the rest. Sylvia told me that Lena had won the top prize two years in a row and was gunning for the top prize this year as well. She sure looked confident as she chatted with friends in the crowd. It was if she knew she had it in the bag.

I couldn't take another bite of a cupcake for the day, so I worked the room, signing a few autographs here and there. It was fun to socialize a bit, since I hadn't talked to anyone aside from my family for a while, unless you counted Aaron...and Sterling.

The sting of imagining Sandra on top of Sterling making out passionately was slowly lessening. Soon, I might even forget it altogether. I hoped.

Chapter 5

The Sunday judging had gone off without a hitch. The contestants came in and baked their cakes in the cooking classroom. We tried them and announced the winner. The news crew from Hartfield's local TV channel was there to film the whole thing. They broadcasted snippets of the event throughout the evening news. I had to do a quick interview as well, talking briefly about my new album.

Unfortunately, another event made it onto the news later that evening: Lena Mumson's murder.

In the end, she did win – third year in a row.

After the contest ended at the school, Lena received her prize, the news crew left, and so did Aaron and everyone else.

It was already dark when we went outside. Once we reached the car, Mirabelle realized that she didn't have her car keys in her purse. We thought that she'd dropped them somewhere, so we unlocked the school door and retraced our steps back to the cooking classroom.

She found the keys on the ground. It was near the table where she'd placed her bag for the majority of the day.

We would've just gone home if I hadn't wanted to pee so badly. I made a quick dash to the girl's washroom. When I opened the door, however, I noticed a trail of blood coming from one of the stalls.

"Hello?" I called out.

I should've turned away, but curiosity got the best of me. The door of the stall was not locked and I nudged it open with one foot.

Then I saw it:

A dead body. Lena. She'd been stabbed in the stomach and she sat limp, slumped beside the toilet.

I screamed.

"Emma?" Mirabelle called from the hallway. "What's going on?"

She came in, but I pushed her out.

"You don't want to see this!" I exclaimed.

"What is it?"

"Lena! She's dead."

I described what I saw and told her to call the police. I was too shaken to hold a phone in my hand, so Mirabelle did the dialling and talking.

We went back outside and sat in Mirabelle's car as we waited for the police.

"I wonder if the killer's still inside," I muttered.

But it wasn't as if I wanted to find out.

"How could this happen?" Mirabelle asked.

"And when?" I thought about it. "Everybody left in the last hour. Lena must've left only half an hour ago. Who would just kill her when there were probably still people around?"

"It must've been someone who really hated Lena. Maybe it was done only in the heat of the moment."

"Right," I said. "It was right after she won, so do you think it could be one of the other contestants?"

"Oh my gosh. It might. I mean, there was no one else in the building except the news crew. And they had gone first. The school is locked. It couldn't be the other two judges. They came out to the cars with us."

"It had to be one of the other contestants then. I don't see why an outsider would come in and kill Lena in the high school washroom of all places. Someone must've been really sore about losing."

"Now who would want the top prize bad enough?" asked Mirabelle.

"Or hate Lena that much."

"Or resent losing one year's worth of hot chocolate at my cafe," Mirabelle joked. I was too horrified to laugh. "Come on. I'm trying to lighten you up."

"You didn't see the dead body," I said. "It was absolutely disgusting. So much blood."

I shivered.

Police car sirens sounded. I dreaded seeing Sterling. And Sandra. Sterling and Sandra together, recalling that scene where they were rubbing against each other at the office. But I took a deep breath. I was a strong woman. I could handle this.

Half a dozen policemen came out. Sterling was there, but Sandra wasn't, luckily. I wondered where she was, but I didn't ask. What did I care?

Sterling strode over to us in his casual clothes: a black wool coat, opened to reveal a gray sweater that matched his eyes. Why did he have to be so handsome?

"Good evening ladies," he said without a smile. Instead he had that smoldering look that I'd always found appealing. But no matter. If he wasn't going to smile, I wasn't going to smile back.

I knew I was being petty. What was there to smile about? There was a dead body in the ladies room.

"Hi Sterling." Mirabelle nodded at him just as coolly. I was glad to have my sister on my side, and literally by my side.

"What happened?"

I told Sterling about staying at the high school a bit later because we were looking for Mirabelle's keys. And then my discovery of the body in washroom. The officer took down some notes and left. Sterling followed him to take a look at the scene.

Mirabelle and I were alone again. She wanted to go home, but something told me to stay. What if they found a clue or something? We could help solve the case.

"Oh, Emma. When I said to keep busy, I didn't mean with another murder case. Haven't you had enough?"

"Come on. They're hopeless at solving these things. They take way too long. I could help. What if this killer strikes again?"

Mirabelle's eyes grew wide. "No, don't get mixed up in this. What if the killer comes after you?"

The sun had set, and it was deadly dark around the school. We looked around.

"We'll be careful," I said, then gulped.

Our house had a security alarm turned on at night. Ever since I came back into town and Mom and Dad realized that I wasn't going anywhere after the holidays as expected, they got the alarm installed in case any crazy fans or reporters tried to sneak in. The town was generally free of paparazzi, but they had descended in the past when word got out that I was in Hartfield.

It must've been about forty minutes later that Sterling came back out.

"Well?" I stepped forward. "Did you find anything?"

Sterling looked impatient. I thought he was going to tell me to go home, but he revealed something.

"As a matter of fact, I did."

Sterling held up a ziplock bag with a small gold hairpin.

"This was in Lena's right hand."

Mirabelle and I both gasped. We both knew who it belonged to, and it wasn't Lena.

Chapter 6

C herry Anderson was the youngest contestant in the top four. She was in her last year of high school, so she knew the premises well. The gold hairpin belonged to her because her corkscrew hair was so unruly that she used a million of those pins to secure the hair in place and keep her curls out of her face.

"We found another in Lena's coat pocket," Sterling said. "Maybe they had been fighting and the pins fell out from Cherry's hair."

"Did you find strands of Cherry's hair in the bathroom?" I asked.

"We did find the type of hair as you described of Cherry's" Sterling said. "Two stalls over, curly blond hair. The washrooms were cleaned by a janitor this morning, although many people have probably been in and out of the bathroom from your crew. There's nobody else with long curly hair, is there?"

"No, Cherry's the only one," I said. "But it could just mean that she used the washroom recently."

"Cherry? A murderer?" Mirabelle shook her head. "She's one of the sweetest girls I know. Comes into my cafe all the time. She wouldn't murder Lena."

Cherry was very nice and smiled often. I remembered that she had been helpful to the other contestants as well, always lending them things, or offering to help if something went wrong. Maybe she thought it was only fair because she was familiar with cooking in those facilities because she went to Hartfield High.

Sterling's expression remained grave. "It doesn't look good. We'll have to take her in."

"There's just no way," Mirabelle said.

"The wound was pretty bad," I said. "You think Cherry really had the strength to do that?"

Sterling shrugged. "Anything's possible. Some people might look weak, but they're not. You just never know with people."

"Yes," I agreed, locking eyes with Sterling. "You just never know with people, do you?"

Sterling turned away.

"We don't have a weapon yet," he said.

"The contestants brought their own tools," Mirabelle said. "And after it was over, they packed up and took them home."

"Which is why we're going to go to Cherry Anderson's house and taking her knives in for testing. She might not have washed all of it off yet. There might still traces of Lena's DNA. Lena's knives were in her bag, still packed and untouched."

Mirabelle shook her head again. "Cherry," she muttered. "No, I just don't believe it."

"It's been a long day, ladies," Sterling said. "Drive home safely. We'll take it from here the rest of the night."

Just then, another car pulled up. A red Corvette. It was Sandra.

She got out in her prim dark coat that matched Sterling's. They should've been related, not dating.

"Come on, Emma, let's go." Mirabelle began unlocking the car.

"Oh, good evening," Sandra said. "Emma, fancy seeing you here. But you're always near the scene of a crime in Hartfield, aren't you?" She chuckled. "It's like that song of yours, 'Trouble Follows Me.'"

"I didn't know you were a fan," I said through gritted teeth.

"Who said I was?" Sandra stepped out of her car in heeled boots. Who wore boots to a crime scene? Did she think she was in a movie?

"Whatever," I said. "Good luck solving the case. You already have the wrong person, by the way."

Sandra's face fell, but she didn't respond. She didn't even know what she was walking into. Having had the last word, I got in the car and Mirabelle drove off.

"Did you see her face?" Mirabelle laughed.

"I don't know what compelled me to say it. Maybe Cherry did do it, I don't know."

Mirabelle shook her head again. "She couldn't have, poor girl. I think you're absolutely right."

"So who did? One of the other contestants? There's Larson and Demi. Do you know anything about them?"

"Hmm." Mirabelle thought about it. "I do know that Demi and Lena had been hugely competitive in the past. In fact, they're pretty much rivals. They used to be best friends in high school, but they grew apart when they started getting more competitive. Last I heard, Lena was still jealous of Demi. Demi had it all – three kids, a husband, a dog, while Lena is still single in her mid thirties with a cat. Maybe Demi couldn't stand the fact that Lena was winning all these contests and going on fabulous vacations every year."

"Seems plausible." I said. "Although is Demi the killer type? She's a soccer mom. Would she be really that mad that Lena won a bake-off?"

"Before the bake-off, Demi was known as the town's best amateur baker. I mean, everyone would dive for her dessert stand whenever there's a fair."

"Oh, is she the one who made those lemon meringue pies that Mom loves so much?"

Mirabelle nodded. "She's the one."

"So she would be peeved to lose her reputation to Lena. Plus they fought over the same boy in high school or something. Maybe there's an even bigger grudge between them than we know."

"It sure doesn't sound good," I said. "Okay, what about Larson?"

"Don't know much about him. This is the first time that he has entered. He's big into sports, so I was surprised when he did enter, and he wasn't half bad either. That Oreo cupcake of his was killer, and his fudge cake? To die."

"You might want to rethink your choice of words," I said with a smile.

"Oh, sorry. Anyway, he used to date Lena for a few years, but they'd broken up last year and now they're both dating other people."

"Well, that sounds suspicious too," I said. "I mean, an ex-lover winning the top prize. And taking a new man on a fabulous vacation to Hawaii? Did he go on the vacations the previous two years?"

"I don't know," Mirabelle said. "We don't keep track once we give out the prizes. That's what the travel agency does. We could ask them."

"Great. Let's ask them first thing tomorrow. Although, we have to make sure that Cherry is innocent. Are you sure she doesn't have some sort of motive?"

"Let's see...she did want a job at my cafe," said Mirabelle. "But my staff was full. I told her I'd keep her in mind for the summer. She really wants to be a baker. She said she was planning on going to culinary school, so she's quite serious and ambitious about this. She told me she must've worked on two dozen recipes before developing and submitting the strawberry cupcakes. And she was also learning how to decorate cakes on her own. She wanted a part-time job so she could save up for college. I liked her and really wanted to help her."

"Wow," I said. "She does sound very determined. What if I was wrong? Maybe she did do it. She sounds like the competitive type. I'll have to look more into her too."

Mirabelle looked at me from the corner of her eye. "This is looking to be a very busy week for you."

"Certainly is," I said. "And I'm supposed to plan this baby shower in the midst of this murder case."

"I'm starting to think that you're staying in town so you can solve these mysteries. You're certainly not staying for Sterling, are you?"

"Oh, Mirabelle, I'm staying to spend more time with you."

"Uh huh."

"Plus, I think I deserve this break from the industry."

Mirabelle parked the car in front of our parents' house and turned off the engine. She faced me to listen to me.

"I think I'm burned out," I said. "Do I really want to be a famous singer forever? Just thinking about doing promotion for this third album is giving me anxiety."

"I didn't know that," Mirabelle said softly. "I thought you were just going through some relationship trouble."

"I thought so too, but I couldn't bring myself to answer Rod's calls about doing interviews. I think he's cancelling a lot of things for me and getting into trouble. But I just can't seem to face it. If I have to go on another talk show and make corny jokes, I swear..."

"Maybe you just want a long hiatus. Not quit."

I nodded. "Exactly. I was ready to start a family, but now I'm single again, so I guess that's what I've been upset about too. Plus there's this reporter following me around. I felt like I couldn't breathe today." I sighed. "I don't know what I want. Maybe I just need to have these distractions. Throw baby showers and do other things that I'm interested in."

"Like criminal investigation?"

"Yes."

"Fine," said Mirabelle. "I think you need this. I'll help you in any way that I can. After all, it is a contest that I'm sponsoring. I can't let the murderer get away with this."

"Okay. Tomorrow, we'll start, but first I'm going to go home and keep working on your baby shower to relax my mind a bit."

Chapter 7

"**H**i, Emma."

I opened the door early Monday morning to see Aaron. Looking cheerful, he held a cup of coffee in each hand.

"Aaron, hi. I thought you were going back to Chicago. Don't you have a deadline?"

"I was," he said, coming inside without even being invited. "But I heard that someone was murdered last night and you were a witness?"

I took his coffee from the Chocoholic Cafe and thanked him. He sure was addicted to my sister's coffee. He had gotten me a chocolate latte, one of my favorite drinks.

"That's right," I said with hesitation. "But maybe I shouldn't be talking about it."

"I was at the cafe this morning, and I heard other people gossiping about it. They said that you found the body."

"Oh no," I said. "How did word get around so fast? I mean, I thought investigations were supposed to stay confidential."

"It is a small town." Aaron shrugged. "I thought word always spread faster in small towns."

"I suppose." I sighed and took a long sip of my latte. Then I briefly explained what had transpired the night before.

"So, are you going to investigate?" Aaron asked.

"What do you mean?" I feigned ignorance.

"Well, I've asked around, and people here seem to know you more for solving murder and kidnapping cases than for being a singer. You've got quite a reputation here."

"I do?" I was surprised. Sure there'd been a write-up or two in the paper when I helped the mayor figure out who had kidnapped his kids last month, but I didn't know that people thought I was some sort of Miss Marple.

"Sure," Aaron said. "So, you're going help figure out who the murderer is, right?"

"Er. I don't know. I mean, I have to fly to Los Angeles soon to appear on a talk show."

"But we both know that you won't," Aaron said with a smile. "Look, I have an extensive background in journalism, sometimes investigative journalism. Maybe I can help."

I looked at him. He really didn't mean any harm. In fact, he looked excited by the prospect of working on a murder case. Maybe he was like me, bored with his daily routine and wanted to do something different.

"Fine," I said. "Can I trust you?"

"Yes, of course," he said. "I won't print anything sensitive in the article about this case."

"Can I have final approval of my article before it runs?"

"Okay" he said. "I have most of it written anyway."

"That was fast." Aaron sure was a professional.

"But I'm looking for something else to add," he said. "A different angle of you that no one else has seen before. An intelligent side."

I laughed. "Thanks a lot!"

Aaron chuckled too. "I'm sorry. I mean, celebrity interviews are always so, *blah*. It's more interesting when I stumble across someone with interests outside of the industry. So crime fascinates you. I can see that from some of the darker imagery in your lyrics, but the fact that you get to solve crimes in real life, well, that could be a real story."

"If we do solve the case, we don't have to write about it in detail, do we?"

"Well, why not?"

"Private investigators stay, well, private."

Aaron frowned. "So really, you just want to be a celebrity who moonlights as an amateur sleuth?"

I nodded. "Exactly. If people know that I'm good at this, they'll be cautious around me."

"Hmm, okay. Fine. We'll cut out the Nancy Drew angle then. But I still want to help you on this case."

I briefed him on everything Mirabelle and I had discussed about who the killer might be, and how we were visiting the travel agency that morning for information. But I told him that I needed help with the Cherry situation. She was being detained at the police station. Evidence was mounting against her, and maybe Aaron could go see what was happening. I certainly did not want to see that Sandra ever again.

"Okay, done," Aaron said. "Cherry Anderson...I'll see what I can dig up at the police station, and I'll find out more about her background."

"Great, thanks. We can meet back at the house later."

After Aaron had gone, Mirabelle came by to pick me up so that we could go to the agency.

"Charles is a friend of mine," she said, referring to the manager at Sunstream Travel. "So hopefully he'll let us know who Lena took on the vacations with her."

"By the way," I said, "I think we have a new ally."

I told her that Aaron was interested in helping us with the case.

"That's great," she said. "As long as we can trust him."

"He says I get final approval on the article, which is nice of him, because they never let me do that."

"Okay." There was doubt in her voice. "As long as he's more of an asset than a hindrance. I just don't trust these reporters. Remember that one woman who pretended she was your long lost BFF, then wrote the most hateful things about you? Horrible. And that other guy who kept trying to hit on you?"

I sighed. "I don't know Aaron that well, but he seems okay. Maybe I'm naive, but we do need the help. Sterling and Sandra are certainly not letting me in on anything, Sandra would make sure of it. I need all the help I can get. The murderer is still out there."

"Okay, okay, I'll trust you on this one."

Sunstream Travel was just off the main street. It was the go-to agency for anyone who wanted to book vacations in this town. While people usually booked vacations online these days, many people in Hartfield were still behind on the times and Sunstream's business was still healthy enough that they could afford to sponsor contests.

"How are you, Charles?" Mirabelle beamed at the man with the red hair and matching red beard sitting at the front desk.

"Mirabelle." He shook her hand. "Lovely to see you, as always. And here's the incomparable Emma Wild. My daughter loves your albums."

"Great," I said. "Always happy to have supporters."

"Sophie only had great things to say about you after meeting you on Emma Wild Day."

"It was nice meeting her too," I said, even though I didn't remember her exactly.

"What can I do for you ladies today?" he asked.

"We're wondering about the winner for the contest," Mirabelle said. "Now that Lena has, well, passed away, who gets the top prize?"

Charles made a scowl. "That's right. I haven't thought of that. A tragedy that something like that could happen. I certainly hope it wasn't over this Hawaii trip."

"Who knows what the motive was?" I said. "I suppose the winner is whoever the runner-up is."

Mirabelle looked at me. "Who is the runner-up anyway? I forgot."

"Let's see, Larson's triple fudge scored second highest, so I guess it was Larson."

"Just out of curiosity, who came third and forth?" asked Charles.

"Demi's strawberry shortcake was third. Cherry's black forest cake was last."

"Curious that Demi wasn't at least the runner-up," said Charles. "She's usually such a good baker. I always make a beeline for her bakery stand at every festival."

"Yes, she's talented," said Mirabelle. "Maybe she couldn't take the pressure of the competition. In the previous years, she'd been in the top two, almost winning, but losing out to Lena each time."

"It's a shame she won't be getting the vacation this year either," Charles said. "But we'll give it to Larson."

"But he's been on these vacations right?" Mirabelle asked casually. "Because he used to date Lena and she had won the previous times. Surely he's bored of them by now."

"Actually, Lena has never taken the vacation option," Charles said.

"What do you mean?" I asked.

"She always chose to take the cash equivalent, so we would just write her a cheque. I expected to write her a cheque this year as well."

"Wow," said Mirabelle. "Who wouldn't want to go to Hawaii?"

"Maybe she needed the money," said Charles.

"Well, we'll be on our way to tell Larson that he has won the free year's worth of hot chocolate," I said. "Would you like us to ask him whether he'll take the vacation or cash?"

"Sure," said Charles. He gave us his business card. "Give him that and when he decides, he can call me here at Sunstream. It probably doesn't feel too great to win like this, so he can call me when he's ready."

"Yes," Mirabelle nodded. "It must be tough, even if she was an ex-girlfriend."

"Well, thanks for your help," I said. "I'll be sure to give Sophie a signed copy of my new album when it comes out."

"That would be great," said Charles. "She'll love that!"

"No problem. Oh and by the way, what is the cash value of the vacation?"

"To Hawaii for six nights, it's around $6700."

Chapter 8

"$6700?" Mirabelle mused when we were outside. "That's some luxury vacation. What would she do with that money?"

I thought about it. "Who knows? Maybe she wants to save up for a bakery or something."

"I don't think so," Mirabelle said. "I overheard her talking to one of the judges. She doesn't want a bakery because it's too much work."

"That's right. I think she has her own online business or something and wouldn't have time for that."

"She's right," Mirabelle. "Thank God my cafe is doing well enough that I can hire people. In the first couple of years, I was working six or sometimes even seven days a week."

"You're lucky," I said. "You don't even have to do much these days."

"Hard work pays off. As you would know. Plus, our chocolate coffee mix is going to start selling in supermarkets next month."

"Congrats!" I said. "It's shaping up to be a great year for you. First the baby, then your own product line? That's really amazing. Oh, and this awesome baby shower that's coming your way."

"How's that going anyway?"

"Great."

"It's not murder-themed, I hope."

"Definitely not. It'll be very cute."

We drove to Larson's house. Mirabelle had his address from his contest application form. Like Lena, he also worked from home. Jobs in Hartfield were pretty limited, so there were some young entrepreneurs in town. Mirabelle said that Larson also had his own online business. He sold cell phone batteries online. It was so successful that it gave him the time to bake, which was what he wrote on his entry form anyway.

His house was a bungalow, fit for a bachelor. When we knocked, he greeted us in his bathrobe. Larson was in his mid to late thirties. Blond and losing his hair in the front, he had a slight beard and a beer belly.

He gave us a big smile and apologized for his attire.

"I wasn't expecting company," he said. "I'm so embarrassed. I just took a shower, which is why I'm not dressed yet. To have Emma Wild in my house too. To what do I owe the honor?"

"We're here to congratulate you on your winnings," Mirabelle said brightly. "I know that under the circumstances, it's a bit difficult to get celebratory here, but you are the second place winner, and so..."

"Yes. I did hear about Lena. It's a real shame. I went over to speak to her boyfriend, Matt, this morning. She has no family here, so it's a tough burden on him with the funeral arrangements and everything."

"Oh, I'm sorry to hear that," I said. "Her parents have passed?"

"Yes," said Larson. "But we've been friends since we broke up, so I wanted to make sure that things were taken care of."

"That's kind of you," said Mirabelle. "Oh and what's that I smell? It's absolutely divine!"

Larson chuckled. "I've been working on my fudge cake recipe. It was passed down from my grandmother, but one of the judges said it was too sweet, so I've been trying to improve on it."

"It wasn't me," I said. "I loved the cake."

"Thank you."

Larson looked down at his robe. "I'm going to change. Would you like to stay here and share a piece of cake with me? It should be ready soon."

"Sure," said Mirabelle.

"Please sit anywhere in the kitchen."

The oven beeped. He put on oven mitts and took out the three cake pans. He turned them onto the racks to let them cool.

"I'll be right back." Larson disappeared up the stairs.

"What do you think?" Mirabelle whispered to me.

I shrugged. "I guess he's okay. Doesn't sound like he has a motive. Maybe we can just find out what Lena has done with the money."

"Okay." Mirabelle was interrupted by a tabby cat strolling along by her feet.

"Hey there," I cooed.

The adorable cat practically smiled. I'd never seen a cat so friendly.

"You are just the cutest." I squatted down to pet the cat. "Where did you come from?"

The cat cozied up to my ankles and purred.

Before long, Larson was stomping back down the stairs, dressed in a blue dress shirt, black pants and dress shoes. The cat disappeared as quickly as it came from the living room.

"You didn't have to get dressed up." Mirabelle laughed.

"Of course I do," Larson said. "A famous singer and the owner of the town's best cafe in my house? I have to look presentable! So, I won the prizes? A year's worth of hot chocolate, huh?"

"And a trip to Hawaii," Mirabelle added.

"But I guess you've been to these all-inclusive vacations with Lena in the past, so you're probably pretty used to it by now, huh?" I watched him carefully.

"Actually, Lena always used to take the cash," Larson said nonchalantly. "Not sure why. I always wanted to go on the vacations, but she just said she needed the money."

"Any idea what for?" I asked.

"Nope."

"Maybe she wanted to invest in something," Mirabelle suggested.

"Nothing I can think of," said Larson. "She makes a good living selling her handicrafts online. Although, I think she mentioned once about making a charitable donation, but she wouldn't tell me what for."

Larson began spreading the fudge frosting over a layer of the cake on a cake stand. We watched, our mouths watering. It was hypnotizing to watch a cake being made. Even though Mirabelle worked with desserts, I could tell she was salivating as much as I was.

Larson's cake had been pretty delicious at the taste test. I might've even voted his the highest, since I was such a big chocolate lover, but Lena won the judges over with originality with her caramel cheesecake, which was just as good, but a bit too sweet for my liking.

He reached into the drawer for a knife to cut the cake. Then he walked back to the fresh cake on the counter. As the blade sliced through the three layers of cake and fudge, it reminded me of Lena's murder. We had to keep focused. We weren't here to enjoy ourselves but to solve a murder case, no matter how delicious and moist the cake looked.

"Here you go." Larson gave us each a huge slice.

"This is delicious," I said. I dug in with my fork and took a huge bite. "So, Larson, were you upset that you weren't able to go on those trips?"

Larson grimaced, but shrugged.

"Well, it was her winnings after all. I couldn't tell her what to do with it. It's not my place."

"But you were together for a while, no?" I asked.

"About four years," said Larson. "But we were too similar, and we both worked from home, which drove each other crazy. I mean, I loved her and thinks she was great as a friend, but we were more like roommates who couldn't stand each other's bad habits after a while. Maybe it was a good thing that we didn't go on those resort vacations. We would've spent 24/7 together on those trips."

He chuckled. Was he chuckling out of nervousness? I thought I saw his hand shake as he lifted the fork from his own piece of cake.

"So who do you think would do this to Lena?" I asked.

"I thought they caught the killer, Cherry Anderson." He shook his head. "Kids these days."

Mirabelle frowned. "How do you know that?"

"I thought it was common knowledge," he said.

"Cherry's a minor," I said. "She wouldn't be reported on the news if she was taken in."

"I heard a bunch of ladies talking about it at the cafe this morning."

Mirabelle sighed. "This town. Does everyone know everything?"

"Yes, well, it's hard to keep a secret for too long here," said Larson. "I don't know much about Cherry. Do you think she did it?"

"No —" Mirabelle said.

"We don't know," I interrupted. "Anything's possible, right? What do you think?"

"Jealous aspiring baker killing a three-time baking champion? It could happen."

"What did you think of their interactions during the bake-off? Was there a lot of tension between them?"

"I don't know," said Larson. "I was so focused on my own recipes that I didn't pay much attention. Cherry did give me some advice about the oven. She was nice, too nice, so that I suspected her of trying to sabotage my work."

"Did she?" Mirabelle asked.

"No, I don't think so. I just thought it was odd that she was so nice and helpful to everyone. Except to Lena, that is."

"Why is that?" I asked.

"Lena got grumpy whenever anyone got in her space, so she must've said something to Cherry. I didn't hear what she said, but her tone wasn't nice."

"How would you describe Lena as a person?" I asked.

"Lena, well...you had to know her to like her. She could be very competitive in certain atmospheres. But she was sweet as a kitten once you got to know her."

"Would you say that she had a lot of enemies?"

"Just whoever got in her path." Larson chuckled again. "But seriously. Sure, there are people who didn't like Lena. She stayed in her own bubble sometimes and didn't like to be disturbed. Heck, she wasn't even talking to me a lot when I made it to the top four with her."

"Why?" Mirabelle asked. "Is she that petty?"

"Like I said, she needed her focus to be the best. There was nothing she liked better than being the best."

"What made you decide to enter the contest this year?" I asked.

"The love of baking," he said. "I've always baked too. That was one of the things I had in common with Lena."

"Would you say you were competitive with her?"

"No. I wasn't anyway. Lena's competitive with everyone."

"So when you entered, you just did it for fun?"

"Yes. In the past, I didn't enter because it was Lena's hobby and I didn't want to compete with her as a boyfriend. But now, why not? We had both moved on with new partners. I liked baking too. Why not have a friendly little competition?"

I smiled. "Yes. And you would finally be able to take a vacation with a girlfriend."

"For sure. Amy's great. We've been seeing each other for four months, but we're already pretty serious."

"Congrats," said Mirabelle. "And to stay friends with a ex too, that takes skill."

"When you live in a small town, you have to stay friends because there's no avoiding them."

Larson chuckled again.

I had asked all I needed to ask...for now. We finished our pieces of cake and thanked him. We gave him Charles's card from Sunstream Travel and passed on the message that he should call to redeem his vacation package.

"Fantastic," said Larson. "Thanks, girls. Come back anytime."

Chapter 9

"That was some cake," Mirabelle said. "I should commission him to bake some for the cafe."

"Let's figure out who the murderer is before we do that," I said.

"What, you think it's him?"

"I don't know," I said honestly. "I mean, he had the right answers for everything. The murderer is always someone you don't expect, right?"

"Except, you are suspecting him, so does that mean he's not guilty?"

"I still don't have the pieces yet," I said. "This money issue might give us a clue. What was Lena doing with it?"

"Suzy works at the bank. Why don't we ask her?"

Suzy was one of Mirabelle's best friends. She came to one of our girls' sleepovers last month and we all had a great time catching up. She was married to her boss at the bank and would probably be able to help us.

"So let's go then," I said.

"It's lunchtime and I'm not hungry," Mirabelle said. "We shouldn't have had so much cake."

Mirabelle called Suzy and asked her if she was at work. Suzy had just been out grabbing a salad but met us back early at the bank. It was perfect timing because she was booked with appointments and meetings all afternoon.

We parked on the street and went inside. Suzy came out to meet us. She was a perky blonde in a baby blue dress suit. When we were growing up, she'd been a frequent visitor to the Wild house, so she knew both of us well.

"How are you girls?" Suzy asked. "Mirabelle, you're even bigger than the last time I saw you."

"Watch it," Mirabelle joked.

"I'm throwing a baby shower for Mirabelle," I said. "Here's the invite."

I gave her the envelope. She opened it and laughed when the baby popped out of the egg-shaped card. "Cute! Of course I'll be there. Come into my office."

Her office was very bare. No window and just a desk and a computer like all the other offices on the hall. The doors were transparent glass so we could see through them. We sat down and Mirabelle explained why we were here.

"Lena Mumson? The woman who got stabbed?"

We nodded gravely.

"We just want to know a tiny piece of information from her banking transactions," I said.

"Oh gosh. Okay. And you're investigating her murder, naturally?" Suzy gave us a wry smile.

Mirabelle pointed to me. "She is. I want very little to do with murder investigations, actually."

"Come on," I said. "You think this is as fun as I do."

"I could be kicking back with a glass of apple juice and reading baby books right now," Mirabelle joked. "But anyway, any idea what Lena would do with that money?"

Suzy did a search. "This information is confidential...but since it is to help find a murderer on the loose, why not?"

She grinned and began typing furiously on her computer. After scrolling through Lena's banking transactions, she found what we were looking for.

"She did deposit a cheque for $6840 from Sunstream Travel around this time last year, and then she made out a cheque a couple of days later for the same amount."

We both peered at the screen.

"To who?" I asked.

"Demi Williams."

"Oh my god," Mirabelle exclaimed.

"And the year before that, the same thing." Suzy said. "It was $6690 then. Also to Demi Williams."

"So every year Lena wins, but gives the winnings to Demi. But why?" Mirabelle furrowed her brows.

"They're either working together or working against each other," I said. "Blackmail?"

Just then my cell phone rang. It was Aaron.

"Let's meet," he said. "I've got some information on Cherry."

Chapter 10

When we drove back to the house, Aaron was already on the porch waiting for us.

"Have you had lunch?" I asked him.

"No," he said with excitement. "I haven't even thought about lunch. I've been busy all morning."

"I'm sure we have something to eat inside," I said. "Come on in."

In the kitchen, I heated up dad's curry stew from last night.

"So shoot," I said. "We have plenty to tell, but you go first."

"Well, the police weren't saying anything. They wouldn't even let me in the building. So I went to the library for a couple of hours to see what I could find on Cherry in the archived newspapers. She's pretty much perfect."

"Perfect?" I wrinkled my nose. "That sounds completely suspicious. Murderers and psychopaths often have a perfect facade. Nobody's perfect."

"Well, she's a straight-A student, always running charitable fundraisers for her high school, and she's very keen on baking. There's even a story in Hartfield High's school paper about her bake sale. Other students participated, but her pies and cakes got their own article because they were so good. She organized the bake sale to raise money for students in Pakistan to receive school supplies."

"I'm telling you," Mirabelle said to me. "Cherry's great. Plus she's super skinny even when she eats all that junk. I would hate her if I didn't like her so much."

"She is eighteen," I said. "Her metabolism is through the roof."

"Cherry said in an interview that her ambition is to ultimately get her own baking show," Aaron continued. "She sounded very ambitious in her interview. She's one of those rare kids who knows exactly what she wants to do and nobody can stop her. I thought it sounded pretty suspect as well. It's plausible that she could've lashed out at Lena from jealousy."

"Is that all you found?" I asked.

"No. I thought I'd try to go back to the station to see if there was anything more I can find out about Cherry and the case. It was impossible, because there were hoards of reporters and TV crews at the front door, but I did catch Cherry's parents sneaking out the back of the police station. At least, I recognized them from one of the pictures in the paper. Her mom had the same corkscrew hair. I followed them in my rental."

"You creep," I joked.

"Yup," Aaron said. "I followed them home and I knocked on their door and told them that I was helping you with the investigation."

"You did?"

"Sure. Like I said, you have a reputation now for detective work. People trust you. Cherry's parents did, and they were more willing to give me more information. They said that Cherry was detained as a suspect and there were no other leads. Things are not looking good because Cherry doesn't have an alibi. She walked home alone that night, and she left around the same time that Lena did."

"All the contestants pretty much left around the same time, didn't they?" Mirabelle asked.

"Yes," I said. "I thought so."

"Anyway," Aaron continued. "They said that Cherry had been upset when she lost and called home when she was packing up. Her eggbeater had malfunctioned, and she'd been stressed out. Her cake had tasted salty and she'd realized that she'd mixed up the sugar with the salt. Then she had to start from scratch, and everything was done in a hurry. Her cake wasn't as good as it could've been. She was really hard on herself."

"Hmm," I said. "Cherry doesn't sound like the type to mix up her ingredients. She's super organized, right?"

"Yes," said Aaron. "I thought the same."

"Foul play," I said. "Somebody was trying to screw up her cake."

"You think it was Lena?" Mirabelle asked.

"There is definitely a Lena-Cherry connection," I said. "After all, why would Lena have Cherry's pins in her pocket?"

"Well, Cherry's hair is so unmanageable that she probably loses them. In fact I found a few at my cafe. She must lose them all the time. It's why she uses the cheap kind. I bet she has a whole box of those pins."

"Now, what would Lena be doing with it?" I thought about it. "It could be that Cherry was the attacker, and Lena had pulled some pins out when she was defending herself...but wouldn't there be more hair in the stall where Lena was, instead of two stalls away?"

"Unless opening the door caused a breeze for the hair to move," said Aaron.

"But Sterling said it was just a couple of strands. It wasn't a clump of hair, which would fall out if they had been in a physical struggle," I said. "If he found a couple of strands, it could've just meant that she just happened to use the washroom sometime in the afternoon that day."

The ringing phone interrupted my string of thoughts. Mom and Dad were both at work, so I went to answer it. The number was unknown on the display and I almost didn't answer it because pesky telemarketers often called at this time of the day. Something compelled me to however, in case it was the police station or someone else with news.

"Hello?"

There was the sound of strong wind.

"Stay out of it," said a muffled voice. *"You and your little sidekick. Stay out of it, Emma Wild. Or off with your head."*

Click.

The caller hung up.

Chapter 11

"What's the matter?" Mirabelle asked with concern.

I must've had a horrified expression on my face. I told them about the phone call.

"Did it sound like a man or a woman?" asked Aaron.

"I don't know," I said. "It was muffled, like someone put a piece of cloth over the speaker to disguise their voice."

"Someone knows you're investigating," Mirabelle said. "And I wonder what they meant by little sidekick. Are they talking about me?"

"It could be me," Aaron said. "I have been doing some snooping around here and asking people a lot of questions. It's hard to be inconspicuous in this town. It's so much easier to be a reporter in a big city."

"Oh God," I said. "I hope I'm not putting you guys in danger."

"You have to call the police," Mirabelle said. "Maybe we can still trace the call."

I took a deep breath. "Right."

Even though calling Sterling was the last thing I wanted to do, I did need his help.

Sterling answered on the first ring. I explained the situation and he sighed.

"So you have been involved," he said. "Emma, this is serious. You can't be poking around with a dangerous murderer on the loose."

"I know, but I need your help in tracing this call. Can you get your guys on it? Just five minutes ago. This person called my house."

"Okay," Sterling said. "But please stop investigating."

"Sterling, doesn't this prove that the murderer is still out there? Doesn't this show that it's not Cherry?"

"Emma, I don't know. It could just be a prank. We're doing a DNA test on Cherry's knife set that she took home with her. We'll find out soon if it's her or not."

"Are you investigating other leads at least?" I asked.

"Emma, that's police business. Please just stay out of it."

Funny, he sounded like the caller.

"Just please call me back as soon as you hear where that call was made from."

"Okay," Sterling said.

I hung up. Now that I thought about it, Sterling and I didn't make a good team. He was too stubborn, never open to exploring the whole picture. He stuck to the obvious; he was more logical.

"I hope he does it," I grumbled to Mirabelle.

"Well we can't let one threat stop us," Aaron said. "Now we still have to figure out why Lena was giving Demi all this money."

"Was it a bribe?" Mirabelle wondered.

"What do we know about Demi?" Aaron asked.

Mirabelle shrugged. "She's a stay-at-home mom. Three sons, so that keeps her real busy. Her husband's a sports teacher at the high school."

"Now what would her motive be?" Aaron asked.

"Maybe she was blackmailing Lena for something," I said. "And this year, Lena didn't want to pay and they got into a struggle."

"But Demi wasn't even second place," said Aaron. "She wouldn't even have the title."

"Unless she was simply upset about losing," said Mirabelle. "But why would Lena have paid her off in the past?"

"Maybe Demi really needed the money for something and Lena wanted to help her out," I said.

"But I didn't think they liked each other," Mirabelle said. "They were a couple of years older than me in high school, but even then I was aware that they had some sort of rivalry going, starting when they fought over the same boy and when Demi got to be Valedictorian and Lena didn't."

"Where would she be now?" I asked.

"At home, probably," Mirabelle said. "Or picking up the boys, or running errands. Shall we go pay her a visit and get to the bottom of this?"

"Sure," I said. "If the three of us go, it won't be so dangerous, especially since the kids are around. She can't harm us then."

Just then, the phone rang again on the home phone. I feared it would be the mysterious caller again, but there was a familiar number on the display.

"Hello?"

"Hey, Emma." It was Sterling, calling from the office. "One of our guys traced the call."

"Oh, great! That was quick."

"It was from a phone booth on Foxmore Street, just across from the elementary school."

"Thanks," I said.

"If you run into any more problems, let me know. But please, I'm begging you, stay out of danger. I doubt you'd find much at this phone booth anyway. Do you need security? We can send some security guards."

"Oh, I'll be fine. But thanks for your concern."

"Emma..."

"Thanks Sterling, I appreciate the information."

I hung up again and told Aaron and Mirabelle this new bit of information.

"Why that street?" I asked.

"There's not a lot of phone booths in town," Mirabelle said. "At least, not a lot of working ones. They're mainly for decoration now that everyone's on cell phones."

"But is it near any of our suspects' homes?"

We took out a map and matched it with the addresses of our three suspects. Cherry lived ten blocks away. Larson lived thirteen blocks away, on the opposite side of town. Demi lived seven blocks away."

"But her sons go to that school," Mirabelle pointed out. "Maybe she was on her way to pick them up and found it convenient to make a quick phone call."

"That's plausible."

"Why don't we go check it out?" Aaron said. "Take a look, and then go question Demi."

"Okay, let's go."

When we opened the front door to go outside, there was a small box on the Welcome mat.

"What's this?" I asked.

"God, I hope it's not a bomb," said Mirabelle.

Aaron's chest puffed up. "I'll inspect it, ladies."

It was a simple small white box and a small envelope was on top. We held our breath as he lifted the lid...

"It's just a cupcake," said Aaron.

It was a red velvet cupcake with cream cheese frosting and little red sprinkles on top in the shape of hearts. The cupcake liner was pink, with little hearts printed on them to match. A heart shaped plastic sign was shoved on top that said "Be Mine" in white letters.

I took the note from Aaron's hand and began to open the envelope.

"Let's see, what it says. *Roses are red, violets are blue, Eat me quickly, and guess who?*"

"Is this a clue?" Mirabelle asked. "I mean, I can't tell if this is from a secret admirer or a death threat."

"What if the cupcake is poisoned?" Aaron asked. "We'll have to get it tested."

"It must be from this caller," I said. "He said 'off with your head', and this cupcake makes a reference to *Alice in Wonderland* too."

"Plus, it's a cupcake," said Mirabelle. "The first round of the contest involved cupcakes."

"Although none of the top four made a red velvet," said Aaron.

"It looks like the murderer is playing a sick, twisted game with me," I said. "I'm certainly not eating it."

"Let's take it to the police," Mirabelle said.

"Fine," I said. "But please, can you do it? I don't think I can talk to Sterling again today."

Aaron looked at me the way reporters did when they thought they had a scoop. "Why? Is he an ex-boyfriend?"

"Let's just stick to the case," Mirabelle gave him a warning look. Then she turned to me. "Okay, I'll drop it off at the station and ask them to get it tested. Let's go. It's after three thirty. Demi should have picked up the kids and gone home already."

Chapter 12

M irabelle came out of the police station empty handed.

"They'll do it," she told us once she was in the car. "They'll test it for poison. That Sandra didn't look too happy to be interrupted, however. Not sure what they're doing exactly. They think this is a nuisance. She made a quip about not having time to look into the stalkers of local celebrities."

"Local celebrity?" I said. "I'm internationally famous."

"Who is Sandra?" asked Aaron. "Does she work at the station?"

"Just another useless detective," Mirabelle said.

"She's not important," I said. "Let's focus on our next task. Demi is our prime suspect right now."

We drove off in Mirabelle's Mini Cooper to Foxmore Street to check out the phone booth first. When we got there, there was a commotion coming from the elementary school across the street.

A soccer game was taking place in the field.

"You think Demi's there?" I wondered out loud.

"Probably," Mirabelle said.

"We're in public," Aaron said. "Even better to approach her here."

"It could've been her then," I said. "She could've just slipped out from the game and made the call. It would've been so easy for her."

"True," Mirabelle said.

We looked at the phone booth. There was nothing inside, no clues, but we looked around at the neighbourhood.

"I'm not sure if anybody would have witnessed who the caller was from their windows," I said. "I suppose we can ask around. But let's talk to Demi first."

We searched for Demi in the stands. She was sitting in the middle of the three rows next to two blond boys. One was around ten and the other was around five.

Mirabelle went down the steps to where she was and spoke to her. Demi looked back at Aaron and me with a grim expression. She stood up, then leaned down to speak to her eldest boy before she followed Mirabelle up to where we were standing. The higher stands were empty and we could talk freely.

"You wanted to talk?" Demi asked.

She looked nervous.

"Yes," I said. "We've been looking into the death of Lena."

Demi nodded. "I figured you would. Do you suspect that I did it or something?"

I looked deeply into her eyes. "Should we suspect you?"

She sighed. "I'm such an obvious suspect. Everyone knows that Lena and I were rivals. But I would never kill her."

"So, do you mind telling us why Lena was paying you the value of the vacations that she won every year at the baking contest?"

Her eyes grew wide. "You know about that?"

"Yes," I said. "Now please answer the question."

"Okay, fine. It's so embarrassing, but Lena was helping me out. Not out of the goodness of her heart, of course. The budget for my husband's sports program was getting cut. Salaries were slashed. Lena knew that if she offered me some money, I would intentionally lose just by a margin in the baking contests so that she could come out the winner."

"What?" Mirabelle exclaimed.

"Yes. She knew that I was the better baker, but she wanted the title. And she knew how desperate I was. We were even going to the food shelter at one point. Once, she saw us coming out of there with two bags of food. I mean, I have three boys. They grow so fast, and we have to pay the mortgage. Sometimes I bake cakes on the side to make money that way, but with three boys, I don't have time, so I just took her money, and lost in the contest. Besides, being second best didn't seem that bad."

"Why does she want to win so badly?" I asked.

"She wanted a book deal," Demi said. "A publisher in Toronto was interested when she approached them after her second win, but they told her they'd draw up a contract only if she won the third contest here in a row. Then that would give her a platform as a three-time baking contest winner in a cozy small town. Otherwise, she would just be a nobody. Who would give a book deal to a nobody?"

"That's all she wanted?" Mirabelle asked.

Demi nodded. "Now, I don't know who killed her, but Lena was very competitive. She did what she could to sabotage the other contestants."

"Why didn't you come forward?" I asked. "To help the police."

"I didn't know what to do. They did have evidence against Cherry, so I figured I'd just let the police do their job. Plus, I was scared. I didn't want them to think that I had something to do with her murder, with this whole money mess."

"You said she tried to sabotage the others?" I asked.

"I don't have proof of that," Demi said. "But Lena was complaining that she was afraid of Cherry overtaking her. Larson she was less scared of, because she knew his capabilities, but Cherry was young and innovative. She was a threat to Lena, so she definitely must've done something to sabotage Cherry if she came last."

"Wow," said Mirabelle.

"So that's why I thought maybe Cherry found out and they had a fight over it. Cherry stabbed Lena and ran. The police got her and I thought the case was over."

"Do you think Cherry did it?" I asked.

"I don't know," Demi said, on the verge of tears.

"But you feel guilty."

She nodded. "I know how mean and difficult Lena can be. If I'd only warned the other contestants, then maybe Lena wouldn't be so hated and dead – now."

"Honestly, we're not so sure that Cherry did it," Mirabelle said. "But Lena had her hairpins."

A thought came to me. "Maybe she picked up the pins and used them to damage Cherry's equipment. Didn't one of you say that her egg beater had malfunctioned?"

Aaron nodded. "I wonder if Lena stuck a hairpin in it to make it malfunction."

"I wouldn't put it past Lena," said Demi. "It sounds like something she would do. After all, it would be Cherry's hairpin, so it wouldn't be traced back to Lena."

"I still don't think it could be Cherry," said Mirabelle. "Once someone at the cafe accidentally spilled hot coffee on her pants, and Cherry was the one apologizing. She's not the type to snap."

"What about Larson?" I asked Demi. "What do you know about Larson?"

"Larson?" she said. "Not much. He and Lena broke up awhile ago. I think Lena complained about who got to keep the cat when they broke up, but that was about it."

"Cat?" I asked.

"Well, I think when they lived together, they kept a cat and Lena wanted to keep it."

"Did she?" I asked.

"I'm not sure."

"Do you really think it's Larson?" she asked. "I don't know him too well, but I always felt sorry for him for putting up with Lena for so long." She pressed her lips together. "Gosh, that's really mean to say, isn't it, now that she's passed away?"

"Wait, what about the phone call?" Aaron pressed. "Emma received a strange call at home today from the phone booth across the street from here."

"A phone call?" Demi asked.

"Yes, a threatening one," I said.

"I swear, it wasn't me. I was with the boys all afternoon. In fact Roddy had a field trip to the science fair and I was one of the parent chaperones. After that, I was here watching the game. I wouldn't be able to leave the boys out of my sight, even to go across the street to make a phone call."

"Fine," said Aaron. "Do you have witnesses? At around 3:30pm."

"Yes," Demi said. "The teachers can tell you that I was here with them, taking the kids back, like I told you."

Her youngest son started crying in the stands below and the older boy was becoming agitated.

"I've got to go," said Demi. "Good luck with the investigation. I'm sorry, but it was humiliating to admit that my family needed help with money. Lena really helped me out and I'm sorry that she was murdered, you know, so if I have to come forward and testify in any way, I will."

We weren't sure whether we hit a wall or we uncovered something new.

But just then, Sterling called with some new information.

Chapter 13

ince my cell phone was still turned off, he called Mirabelle's phone.

"So the cupcake is just a cupcake," said Sterling. "It's red velvet with cream cheese frosting."

"Really?" I asked.

"It's your favorite flavor, isn't it?" Sterling asked.

"I suppose," I said. "Who would know that?"

"Maybe you stated it in an interview once."

"Okay, but are you sure there's no poison?"

"No. Our guy said that it would've been detectable right away, but this is the perfect cupcake. Freshly baked, too."

"Sounds good," I said.

"It's probably from a die-hard fan," said Sterling. "With a crush. I'll throw the cupcake away. Do you want the note?"

I sighed. "Sure. Keep it. Maybe it'll come in handy. Did you find out anything new?"

Sterling was silent for a moment. I could tell he was contemplating whether to tell me or not.

"Not yet. Except we did get part of the autopsy report back. She'd been sliced from the stomach up to the rib cage. There *was* a knife involved. We're still waiting for Cherry's results for her knife, so hopefully we'll get an answer soon."

"Okay, thanks."

"Look, I've got to go," Sterling said.

"Go then," I said. "Thanks for the report."

He hung up. Although the cupcake clue went nowhere, the way Lena was killed with a knife stirred some suspicions in me...I had an idea who did it, but I didn't have proof.

"Hey Emma?" Mirabelle called from the living room. "I've got to go to the cafe. Cal is having trouble with the debit card machine."

"Okay," I said. "I'll just continue on with Aaron then."

"The cafe's so close and it's faster if I walk, so I'll leave you guys the car."

"Thanks."

After she left, I filled Aaron in on what Sterling had told me.

"We have to go visit Lena's boyfriend," I said. "I heard he was gone during the bake-off on a business trip. But he's in town now."

Aaron nodded and grabbed his bag. We were off in the Mini Cooper to Lena's house. They were living together, so we knew where the house was. Lena had mentioned her boyfriend a few times during the weekend. He had lived in a nearby town, and they'd met through an online dating site. He'd moved in with her, but he traveled regularly around Canada for business.

We were just about to knock on the door when we heard voices from the inside.

Two men were yelling at each other.

"Please, put it down," one man was saying. "I promise. I won't tell anyone. You have my word."

"But is your word good enough?" growled another voice.

Just then, Aaron slipped off the porch and made a huge noise. He was holding his ankle in silence while his face expressed nothing but pain.

There was silence from the inside of the house as well. Then I heard whispering.

A man with dark hair and a fearful expression poked his face out the door.

"Can I help you?" he asked.

I was helping Aaron up, who was able to stand.

"Are you Matt?" I asked.

"Yes," he replied.

"Is everything okay? We heard yelling."

"Everything's fine," he said. "Is your friend okay?"

"It's my ankle," said Aaron. "I don't think it's broken, thank God. It's a little sprained, but I think I'll be fine."

"Can I help you with something?" Matt asked.

"Yes," I replied. "We're here to see you, but is everything is okay? We heard screaming."

"I have company over," he said. "Can you come back another time? I'm afraid I'm in the middle of something."

His face expressed nothing but fear. His voice quivered. He slammed the door shut and we heard a locking sound.

"That was weird," Aaron said.

We heard more noises, shuffling, grunting. Someone was coming out the back.

I ran around to the side of the house and saw him. Larson! He was jumping over the fence and running away.

I went inside the house from the back porch and found Matt lying on the floor with a huge gash on one of his arms.

"Oh my God!" I exclaimed. "Are you okay?"

"Call an ambulance," he said. "I feel faint."

"Yes."

I made the call and got some tea towels from the kitchen for the blood that was pouring from his arm.

"It was Larson, wasn't it? I saw him run away."

Matt nodded. "Yes, it's him."

I called Sterling next.

"Did he drive here?" I asked Matt.

"No," said Matt. "Well, I don't know, but I think he came by foot. Snuck in the house through the back."

Sterling picked up.

"Emma? What —"

"Sterling, listen, the murderer is getting away. It's Larson. He's running from the back of Lena's house. I think he's on foot, but he might have a car. You better send all your guys to arrest him right away. He tried to kill Lena's boyfriend just now."

"Wow, okay —"

I hung up and got Matt a glass of water.

"He's crazy," Matt said. "So you know he killed Lena too?"

I nodded. "Well, I suspected him, and I was just on my way here to ask you about Lena's cat. They fought over it and I thought it could've been a driving force behind this murder."

"Well, Lena's cat went missing when I came home from my business trip," Matt said. "Then I saw Larson buying cat food at the pet shop and I got suspicious. They had fought about this cat that was really Lena's pet. Larson gave it to her for her birthday or something. I thought maybe he had the cat and I'd called him to ask about it. He said he knew nothing about it. I went over there this afternoon to ask him about it again. I didn't see the cat, but he got aggressive. Too aggressive. He completely denied having the cat. I'd always thought he was a pretty decent guy. He even came over yesterday to ask me if I needed help with Lena's funeral, so it was strange to see him so worked up about a cat today."

"Maybe he realized he couldn't get out of the lie this time," I said, "because we'd been at his house this morning and we saw the cat. He probably got paranoid."

"Yes, and he came over now with the knife, threatening to kill me. I think he's a little crazy. He's just not right in the head. There was a crazy look in his eyes."

Chapter 14

"How did you figure out who the killer was?" Sterling asked me.

I was down at the police station, filling out a report about Larson. When they caught Larson, there was blood on his shirt. He was running towards the woods, just trying to get as far from the town as possible. He knew that we had figured it out.

He had been close to killing Matt before Aaron and I got there. When he realized that Matt couldn't be killed on the spot without killing Aaron and me too, since we were witnesses, he fled.

"When you told me about Lena's autopsy," I said. "I had this big hunch that it was Larson."

"Why?"

"Because this morning we had been at his house to give him his Chocoholic Cafe gift card for being the runner-up. He was making a cake, and he cut us each a slice. When he took out a knife from the drawer, he walked from the drawer back to the counter where we were sitting and I noticed that he had gripped it with the sharp end of the knife facing upwards. It was the natural way he held a knife. And when you said that the murderer had cut Lena upwards to her stomach, I could imagine him thrusting the knife into someone and ripping upwards."

"Okay." Sterling nodded stoically. "But why did you go to Lena's house?"

"To talk to her boyfriend," I said. "Demi said Lena and Larson used to fight over the custody of this cat that they owned when they used to live together. I saw a tabby cat at Larson's house, so I wanted to ask Matt whether it was Lena's. I wanted to see if this cat was a motive in the murder."

Sterling shook his head. "I've never seen a guy get so worked up about a cat. He has mental issues. In the interrogation room, he confessed, ranting about how Lena broke his heart, destroyed his life and kept the only other thing that he loved: his cat. He was upset that she would shove her new boyfriend in his face. He wanted to get back at her by winning the contest, but when Lena won again, he got upset. He claimed that she taunted him with taking her new boyfriend on vacation with her."

"What about his current girlfriend?" I asked.

"There is no girlfriend," he said. "He claimed to have a long-distance girlfriend, but it turned out that he was just saying that to make Lena jealous. He also thought he had a strong chance in winning the contest, but I suppose Lena knew that he didn't. Valentine's Day was their anniversary. I suppose this could also be a crime of passion. Larson couldn't stand the thought of Lena being with her new boyfriend and keeping their cat, while he was alone. He said that she was really rubbing the vacation thing in his face, telling him how happy she was that she had it all – the boyfriend, the prize, the vacation and how she was going to get a book deal."

So she was probably going to stiff Demi on her money too.

"Larson's going to plead insanity," Sterling said.

"Why did he send me the cupcake?" I asked.

"He said he didn't know anything about it. I told you, it's probably from some fan."

Before I could ask him more questions, Sandra came in, holding two cups of coffee. She passed one to Sterling with an adoring look on her face.

"Hello, Sandra," I said cheerily.

"Emma." She put on a fake smile. "Congrats on finding the murderer."

"You're welcome," I said a little too smugly. "I'm just glad an innocent person like Cherry can go free now. She could've had her life ruined for a wrongful conviction, you know."

"Well, the DNA on her knife didn't come back with anything, so we didn't have anything on her anyway," Sandra said quickly.

"But I'm sure you were just doing your jobs," I said. Even if you were doing it terribly, I wanted to add, but I bit my tongue.

"I'm sure we would've found out that it was Larson in the end," Sandra said.

"Sure," I said. "After he killed Matt, right?"

Sterling looked embarrassed. He cleared his throat. It was my cue to leave.

"If you'll excuse me, I have a baby shower to plan."

Chapter 15

On a Sunday afternoon, Mirabelle, Suzy, Mom, and ten more of our closest female friends were competing to see who could suck beer out of the baby bottles the fastest. Mirabelle, being pregnant, stuck with apple juice. Mom won.

Mom could drink anyone under the table. I gave her the prize of a $50 gift certificate to the town's wine store and she yelped in glee.

Then we played "pin the sperm on the uterus," a game I made out of pieces of felt and Velcro. It was a hit. We had to pin each sperm blindfolded and the one pinned closest to the egg on the uterus won.

After that, we spent a good hour decorating onesies for the baby.

It was such a blast that, before I knew it, the shower was over. I had successfully pumped up the competitive spirit in everyone by giving out great prizes to fight over, like gift certificates and chocolate baskets.

The men had been banished from the Wild house. Dad got kicked out to Mirabelle's house to join her husband, and they had their own version of the shower – drinking beer and watching hockey on TV.

Mirabelle was thrilled with the shower. She told me that I should probably become some sort of party planner.

It had been a pretty eventful week.

Aaron's ankle healed. He felt stupid for slipping off the porch step, but ultimately it was for the best, because otherwise Larson would've killed Matt.

Before he left, Aaron let me read the article that would run in Rolling Stone. I loved it. It made me sound human and flawed, unlike other interviews that either glorified me or bashed me. He wrote about my small town interests, my vulnerabilities, and how I was aware of my own flaws but accepted them nonetheless. Aaron said it was his most in-depth celebrity interview, and he was proud of it, even if he didn't get to include the juicy stuff about solving a murder case together.

Cherry was released, of course, and Mirabelle split the final winnings between her and Demi. They had the option of taking the vacation...together, but they took the money because they both needed it.

The police checked, and yes, they did find one of Cherry's pins in the blender. Cherry was shocked that Lena would stoop so low to win, but maybe it toughened her up a little. Since Cherry ultimately wanted to work in TV, I told her that this experience had probably been good preparation for the industry.

After the shower was over and all of the girls went home, including Mirabelle, Mom and I were home alone. She went into the kitchen to start on dinner when the doorbell rang.

I went to answer it. When I looked through the peephole, I was shocked. It was Nick!

I opened the door to see him holding a bouquet of roses and a cupcake.

"Surprise!" he said.

"Nick?" I grinned from ear to ear.

"I know you hate surprises, but somehow you love mysteries."

I took the cupcake that he offered, the same kind that had been left on my porch.

"It was you?" I exclaimed.

"You didn't guess that it was me?" Nick frowned.

"I thought it was from the murderer."

"What murderer?"

"Oh? You haven't heard?"

"No. There's been another murder here?"

I quickly explained.

Nick shook his head. "Geez. No. On our second date, we shared a cupcake at Serendipity, remember? I had the same cupcake shipped from New York."

"Oh my gosh." My hands went over my mouth.

"In a couple of hours, it's going to be midnight. Valentine's Day. I was wondering what you were doing on that day? Do you have a date?"

"Oh, is it tomorrow?" In the midst of all the chaos, I'd forgotten. "I'm not doing anything."

"Really? Not even with that cranky detective?"

I smiled. "Not a chance."

"Then I have a special date planned for you."

"But why didn't you call?"

Nick shrugged. "I thought it would be more fun to drop in and see you in person. Aren't you glad to see me?"

"Yes. So, you're not with Chloe Vidal?"

Nick laughed. "Why would I be? You actually believed those rumors? Chloe's become a good friend after the shoot. She's like a little sister to me. Plus she's bisexual and in a relationship with the set decorator."

"Oh." I felt stupid. "Why do I always believe the hype about you in the papers?"

I hugged him and he leaned in and gave me the sexiest kiss.

"Come on, if I believed everything I read about you, I wouldn't sleep at night. There was one last week saying that you had been seen leaving John Mayer's apartment."

"That is such crap," I exclaimed. "You know I've been here the whole time."

"I know," Nick said. "Why are you still here? Isn't your album coming out?"

"Um, I'm still taking a hiatus."

"Sounds good. As long as we're doing it together."

"I'm just so surprised that you're here. I thought you'd moved on or something."

"I told you I wanted to marry you." Nick winked. "You should believe me by now."

I guess I couldn't. Nick Doyle to me still wasn't quite real. In fact, even seeing him in front of me, I still had the feeling that he only existed on movie screens. He was a living legend.

He was only real every time he kissed me.

And he did, again and again on the porch, to prove his existence.

Chapter 16

On Valentine's Day, Nick did surprise me all right. In a rental car, he drove me to the countryside where a group of huskies waited for us in the snow. After we shared a glass of champagne from the trunk of the car, we were off on a sleigh ride with the huskies!

It was the most fun Valentine's Day I'd ever had. Every year, Nick made the effort to plan something adventurous but romantic. Last year, we'd gone scuba diving in the Bahamas and had a romantic dinner for two by the sea.

I realized that although Nick did travel and work a lot, he always remembered birthdays, holidays and special occasions, and he put his all into planning special dates for us to experience together. He was a romantic and he loved me. And actions spoke louder than words.

"I hoped I'd given you enough space," he said.

"Space?"

"You know, to think about you and me. The fact that you're not with Sterling tells me that he's history. I always knew that he was a rebound."

I playfully punched him on the arm. "You're so smug. Sterling and I had a history, and I guess I thought we still had something, but coming home wasn't as easy as I thought. It's like trying to relive your youth. I'm too old for that now. Sterling and I are not compatible."

"I always knew you were only right for me." Nick hugged me close.

I pulled back. "There are still things I want, of course, like taking it easy and starting a family. Are you sure that's what you want?"

"Yes," said Nick. "You know that you're the longest relationship I've ever had? I'm so sorry that I had to lose you for a while to realize that you're the one I want to be with for the rest of my life. I'm starting to get up there too, and I do think it's time to talk about kids. I think I would make a pretty good father."

I play-punched him again. He sure was arrogant, but what did you expect from a movie star?

He pulled out a box from his coat pocket. It was the same box with the same big diamond that I had caught a glimpse of on Christmas.

Nick bent down on one knee, in the pure white snow, in the middle of nowhere.

A cry escaped my lips. Of joy. Nick looked up at me eagerly waiting for one word.

And I gave it to him.

Yes.

Lena's Lavender Cupcakes with Lemon Frosting

Makes around 12-15 cupcakes.

- 1/2 cup whole milk
- 1 cup all-purpose flour
- 1 tsp baking powder
- 3 tbsp dried culinary lavender
- 3 tbsp softened unsalted butter
- 1 egg

Lemon frosting:
- 4 cups confectioner's sugar
- 1/2 cup softened butter
- 1 tsp pure lemon extract
- Finely grated zest of 1 lemon
- 4 to 5 tsp lemon juice

Combine the milk and dried lavender in a bowl with a lid on top and leave it in the fridge for 6 to 8 hours, or overnight, to infuse.

Preheat oven to 325 degrees F.

Butter, egg and infused milk need to be at room temperature. Line your cupcake pan with cupcake liners. Use a strainer to remove the dried lavender from the infused lavender milk.

In a bowl, sift together the flour, baking powder and salt. Add sugar and softened butter. Mix well (with stand mixer or handheld mixer) until texture is sandy.

With the mixer on low, slowly add the milk into the mixture. Then add the egg. Mix for 15 seconds on medium speed, then scrape the sides and bottom of the bowl to make sure everything is combined. Just don't overmix, as that will result in a dry cake.

Fill each liner 2/3 full. Bake for 20-30 minutes or when a toothpick comes out clean. Remove cupcakes and set on a wire cooling rack until completely cool.

Frosting: Mix the butter with the sugar. Add lemon extract, zest and lemon juice, beating on low speed until smooth. Increase mixer speed to medium and continue beating for around 2 minutes. Add more sugar if needed for spreading consistency.

Demi's Classic Vanilla Cupcakes with Buttercream Frosting

Makes around 12-15 cupcakes.

- 1/2 cup all-purpose flour
- 1 cup sugar
- 3 large eggs
- 3/4 cup milk
- 1 tsp baking powder
- 1/2 tsp salt
- 8 tbsp (1 stick) unsalted butter, room temperature
- 1 1/2 tsp pure vanilla extract

Frosting:

- 1 cup unsalted butter, room temperature
- 2 1/2 cups powdered sugar
- 1 tbsp vanilla extract

Preheat the oven to 350 degrees F.

Line your cupcake pan with paper liners.

In a bowl, sift together the flour, baking powder and salt.

In another bowl, cream together the butter and sugar until light and fluffy. Add eggs, one at a time, and then beat in vanilla. Alternate adding the flour mixture and milk, beginning and ending with the flour mixture.

Fill each liner 3/4 full. Bake until golden, around 20 minutes, rotating the pan once if needed. Transfer to wire rack; cool completely.

Frosting: Whip the butter on medium-high speed for 5 minutes, stopping to scrape the bowl once or twice.

On low speed now, slowly add the powdered sugar. Then increase the speed to medium-high and add vanilla. Whip until light and fluffy, about 2 minutes, scraping the bowl as needed.

You can store any unused frosting in the fridge in an airtight container. Take it out when needed and let sit until it's at room temperature, and then give it a quick whip before using.

Cherry's Strawberry Cupcakes with Strawberry Whipped Cream

Makes around 12-15 cupcakes.

- 1 2/3 cup + 1 tbsp all-purpose flour
- 4-5 large strawberries
- 1/2 tsp baking powder
- 1/4 tsp baking soda
- 1/2 tsp salt
- 1 cup granulated sugar
- 1/2 cup unsalted butter, melted
- 1 large egg
- 1/4 cup strawberry yogurt
- 3/4 milk
- 1 tsp vanilla extract

Strawberry Whipped Cream:

- 1 1/2 cups heavy whipping cream

- 3 tbsp granulated sugar

- 1 and 1/2 tsp vanilla extract

- 1/3 cup strawberry jam

Preheat oven to 350 degrees F. Line pan with cupcake liners.

Slice strawberries. Use a food processor or blender and pulse until they are a chunky puree.

In a medium bowl, mix together flour, baking powder, baking soda and salt. Set aside

In a large microwave-safe bowl, melt butter in the microwave. Stir in sugar. Mixture will be gritty. Stir in egg, yogurt, milk and vanilla extract until all is combined.

Slowly mix dry ingredients into wet ingredients until no lumps remain. Fold in the strawberry puree. Batter will be thick! Should be enough to divide between 12 cupcake liners.

Bake for 20 minutes or when toothpick comes out clean. Transfer to wire rack; cool completely.

Strawberry Whipped Cream: In a large bowl, whip the cream, sugar and vanilla extract together on high speed until stiff peaks form, about 4-5 minutes. Add the strawberry jam and beat for another 30 seconds. Add more jam if you want a stronger flavor or a pinker color. However, the more jam you add, the thinner the whipped cream will be. Cover and store cupcakes in the fridge for up to 3 days. Serve cupcakes chilled.

Larson's Lazy Fudge Oreo Cupcakes

Makes around 12-15 cupcakes.

- 1 regular package Oreo cookies
- 1 package chocolate cake mix

Frosting:

- 1/2 cup butter
- 8 ounces cream cheese, room temperature
- 1 tsp vanilla extract
- 3 3/4 cups powdered sugar
- 1 package Mini Oreo cookies for decoration (optional)

Preheat oven to 350 degrees. Mix packaged cake mix according to box directions (but do not bake). Line cupcake pan with liners. Place a regular Oreo at the bottom of each liner. Take half of the remaining cookies to chop coarsely and add to the cake mixture. Fill the cupcake liners. Bake for 15 minutes (or time on box directions).

Frosting: Cream butter and cream cheese together. Add vanilla, then powdered sugar slowly until blended well. Chop remaining regular sized Oreos finely (or put them in the food processor) and add to frosting.

When the cupcakes have cooled, frost and decorate with Mini Oreos.

Surprise Red Velvet Cupcakes

Makes around 12-15 cupcakes.

- 1 cup flour
- 3 1/2 tbsp pure cocoa powder
- 1/2 tsp baking soda
- 1/4 tsp salt
- 1/3 cup and 1 tbsp butter, softened
- 3/4 cup + 2 tsp sugar
- 1.5 eggs
- 1/3 cup + 1 tbsp sour cream
- 3 tbsp + 1/2 tsp milk
- 1 ounce red food coloring
- 3/4 tsp pure vanilla extract

Vanilla Cream Cheese Frosting:

- 3/8 (8 ounce) package cream cheese, softened
- 1 tbsp and 1 3/4 tsp butter, softened

- 2 1/2 tsp sour cream

- 3/4 tsp pure vanilla extract

- 3/8 (16 ounce) box confectioners' sugar

Preheat oven to 350 degrees F. Mix flour, baking soda and cocoa powder in a medium bowl.

In a large bowl, beat butter and sugar with electric mixer on medium speed for 5 minutes or until light and fluffy. Beat in eggs. Mix in sour cream, milk, food color and vanilla. Gradually beat in flour mixture on low speed until blended. Do not overbeat. Fill cupcake liners 2/3 full.

Bake for 20 minutes or until toothpick comes out clean. Cool completely.

Frosting: Beat cream cheese, butter, sour cream and vanilla until light and fluffy. Gradually beat in sugar until smooth. Frost cupcake.

About the Author

Harper Lin lives in Kingston, Ontario with her husband, daughter, and Pomeranian puppy. When she's not reading or writing mysteries, she's in yoga class, hiking, or hanging out with her family and friends. She lived in Paris in her twenties, which inspired *The Patisserie Mysteries*.

She is currently working on more cozy mysteries.

www.HarperLin.com

CPSIA information can be obtained
at www.ICGtesting.com
Printed in the USA
BVHW032154011219
565348BV00001B/35/P